NOTHING TO DO

By Liza Alexander/Illustrated by Tom Cooke

A SESAME STREET/GOLDEN PRESS BOOK

Published by Western Publishing Company, Inc., in conjunction with Children's Television Workshop.

"It's a perfectly glorious day!" said Granny Bird to
Big Bird as they finished breakfast. "Go and play
outside. Shoo, shoo!"

Granny's backyard was usually one of Big Bird's
favorite places. Most days he liked to make mud pies
by the flower garden, but today the mud was all
caked and hard. He loved to play on his own special
swing, but today there was no one to push him.

Big Bird was bored. "Granny Bird," he called,
"there's nothing to do!"

"Nonsense!" said Granny. "There's plenty to do out there. Why don't you go see how the fish are doing?"

Granny had a little pond with stones around the edge and a lily pad in the center. Big Bird went over to it and said, "Hello, goldfish." The fish just kept on flapping their fins back and forth and puffing their gills in and out.

Big Bird tried skipping stones across the pond. He tossed a flat stone and it made two skips on the water. The second stone fell plop into the water without skipping at all. Big Bird looked up at the sky and let out a long sigh.

Granny called out the window to Big Bird, "Be a good bird, now, and pick some flowers for the kitchen table."

Big Bird picked a bunch of daisies and brought them to Granny. The screen door creaked as he opened it and thwacked as it slammed shut.

Granny shook the suds off her rubber gloves and arranged the daisies. Big Bird watched. "Now, dear," said Granny, "would you like to help wash the dishes?"

Big Bird gave a big yes. Doing the dishes made him feel grown up. He wiped each dish dry without a drip and stacked them.

When they had finished washing the dishes, Granny said, "No rest for the weary! It's baking time."

Granny asked Big Bird to help her sift the very best birdseed for a pie. She showed him how to use the rolling pin and how to pinch the edges of the dough together.

Then Granny let Big Bird press
a fork all over the top crust.
It made marks like a little bird's
footprints on the beach.
"Neat!" said Big Bird.
As Granny put away her oven mitts
Big Bird sat down again and slumped
lower and lower into his chair.
"Granny, what can I do now?"
he asked.

"Well, dearie, there's plenty of laundry to wash," said Granny.

She taught Big Bird how to sort the clothes into four different piles. Then she let him pour the soap into the washing machine and turn it on.

Before Big Bird had time to get bored again, Granny plunked a plate down in front of him and said, "Time for lunch!"

After birdseed sandwiches and sarsaparilla soda, the wash was ready to be hung up to dry. Big Bird liked the fresh smell of the damp laundry and how the clothespins closed with a snap.

Granny yawned and said, "Oh, dear,
I'm tired. It's time for my nap!"
As Granny went upstairs
she said, "You'll have to
entertain yourself now,
Big Bird."

"Ho hum," said Big Bird. He dragged Radar out to
the backyard. They lay down on the grass and
watched the clouds roll across the blue sky. "Radar,
you look hungry. I guess it's time for your tea!"

In the hollow of the oak tree Big Bird found some acorns that made just the right teacups. Then he gathered some twigs for spoons. A tulip that had fallen from its stem made a perfect sugar bowl.

"Look at this!" Big Bird said to Radar. "Here's our teapot." It was Granny Bird's watering can.

"We'll need some plates," he said and put two big flat leaves on the table. "There, that's that."

"Oh, my goodness, Radar!" said Big Bird. "You're hungry and I forgot the food. I'll go make some now."

Big Bird had a bright idea. He brought the watering can over to the flower patch and poured some water on the caked-up mud. Soon the mud was nice and doughy, and Big Bird could make his special mud pie. When it was baked, he brought it over to Radar, who looked pleased.

"Wait," said Big Bird. "We need some flowers." He chose a couple of fuzzy yellow dandelions to decorate the tea table.

Big Bird and Radar pretended to eat the pie. "All gone," said Big Bird. "Now it's time to wash the dishes."

Big Bird took Radar and the dishes over to the birdbath. Then he dragged a garden chair over for Radar to stand on so he could help. Big Bird washed, Radar dried, and they set out all the dishes in the sun.

"What can we do now, Radar?

"Radar," cried Big Bird, "you got pie on your shirt! Oh, dear! Let me wash it for you now."

Big Bird took Radar's shirt over to the pond and washed it. "Look at the goldfish, Radar," he said. "They're just swimming around, looking bored. I guess they have nothing to do!

"Oh, boy!" said Big Bird to Radar. "I'm tired, aren't you? Let's take a nap." The bird and the bear curled up on a nice soft patch of moss under a tree.

Big Bird pretended to snooze. After a few moments, he sat up and stretched his wings. "Yessirree, nothing like a little nap in the afternoon to refresh a bird. But what can we do now?

"I've got an idea, Radar," said Big Bird. "Let's swing!"

Big Bird put Radar on the swing. He gave Radar one push and then another. The swing went back and forth, back and forth.

By the time Granny Bird came down from her nap, the swing was swooping up and down, up and down.

"Oh, Big Bird!" said Granny. "It looks like you and Radar are having fun!"

"We sure are," said Big Bird as he pushed Radar higher and higher. "But we have nothing to do!"